Get ready for mall madness!

Mom took two plastic badges out of the desk drawer. "Here. I made these store name tags for you."

"Cool!" Jessica said as Mom pinned a tag on her dress.

"Awesome!" I said. Our name tags were just like the ones Mom and Mrs. Hengstler wore. My tag had Elizabeth Wakefield printed in big black letters under the store's name. I was so proud!

Mom motioned for us to follow her. "OK, girls. Now you're official Taylor's employees. It's time for me to show you the Home department."

Jessica and I giggled at Mom's official-sounding tone. She was treating us like real salespeople!

Bantam Books in the SWEET VALLEY KIDS series

DANGER: TWINS AT WORK!

Written by
Molly Mia Stewart

Created by
FRANCINE PASCAL

Illustrated by
Marcy Ramsey

BANTAM BOOKS
NEW YORK · TORONTO · LONDON · SYDNEY · AUCKLAND

RL 2, 005-008

DANGER:TWINS AT WORK!
A Bantam Book | May 1998

*Sweet Valley High® and Sweet Valley Kids® are
registered trademarks of Francine Pascal.*

Conceived by Francine Pascal.

*Produced by Daniel Weiss Associates, Inc.
33 West 17th Street
New York, NY 10011.*

Cover art by Wayne Alfano.

ISBN: 0-553-48615-2

Published simultaneously in the United States and Canada

*Bantam Books are published by Bantam Books, a division of Bantam
Doubleday Dell Publishing Group, Inc. Its trademark, consisting of the
words "Bantam Books" and the portrayal of a rooster, is Registered in the
U.S. Patent and Trademark Office and in other countries. Marca
Registrada. Bantam Books, 1540 Broadway, New York, New York 10036.*

PRINTED IN THE UNITED STATES OF AMERICA

OPM   0 9 8 7 6 5 4 3 2 1

To Louis Duszynski

CHAPTER 1
Career Day

"Class, tomorrow is Take Our Daughters to Work Day," Mr. Crane said. "I know you girls will have fun learning about your parents' jobs. And so will the boys who choose to take part in it."

"Yeah, and the rest of us will have fun at school without the *girls* for a day," Charlie Cashman said with a grin.

Jessica flipped her hair over her shoulder. "Well, we won't have to put up with you *boys* either."

I laughed, and Jessica smiled proudly.

By the way, I'm Elizabeth Wakefield. Jessica's my twin sister. She doesn't like boys very much. Jessica and I are both in Mr. Crane's second-grade class at Sweet Valley Elementary, and we look exactly alike. We have long blond hair with bangs and blue-green eyes.

Even though we're twins on the outside, we're totally different on the inside. I like to play soccer with the boys, but Jessica likes to play dress up with the girls. She's the best jump roper in the class, though, and she's a great speller. But her favorite part of school is recess. Me, I like school—even homework. I usually hate missing a day, but tomorrow is special. Jessica and I will get to spend the whole day with our mom at her new job. I can't wait!

"When you come back to school, each of you can talk about your day at

2

work," Mr. Crane announced. Then he called on Ricky Capaldo.

"If we're not going to work with our parents, can we play softball instead?" Ricky asked.

Mr. Crane laughed. "I'm afraid not, guys. We're going to visit the library and look at books about different jobs. You'll choose a book to read in class and tell everyone about it when we have share time."

"We get to read when they get the day off," Ken Matthews complained. "Forget it. I'm going to work with my dad."

"Me too," Todd Wilkins said. "Maybe he'll let me use his computer all day. Or I can make copies for him on the copy machine."

"Computers? That's no fair," Andy Franklin whined. "I'm going to my mom's bakery."

"You'll look real cute in an apron," Charlie teased.

Winston Egbert leaned back in his desk chair. "Guess what I'm going to be when I grow up," he said.

"A doofus," Charlie joked.

"A clown?" Caroline Pearce asked.

"A zookeeper," Jerry McAllister said. "You'd fit right in with the wild animals."

Winston shook his head. "I'm going to be a mortician."

"Morticia? Wasn't she in *The Addams Family*?" Sandy Ferris asked.

"I said a *mortician*," Winston repeated. "You know, one of those guys who wears black and takes care of dead people."

"Ooh, creepy," Jessica said.

Winston sat up straight and crossed his arms over his chest. *"I want my mummy,"* he said in a low voice.

Mr. Crane laughed along with us. "Well, what would the rest of you like to be when you grow up?" he asked.

"A professional soccer player," Todd said.

"A fireman," Kisho Murasaki added.

"A veterinarian," Ellen Riteman said.

"A cop," Charlie said. "A real tough guy."

"A karate teacher," Julie Porter offered.

"A bug scientist," Andy said.

Jessica rolled her eyes. "I'm going to be a movie star."

"I'll be a writer like my favorite author, Angela Daley," I said. I love to write poetry and read.

"I'll be a dancer and a model," Lila Fowler said. "And I'm going to live in

Paris with my mother. I'll be famous and be on magazine covers."

Jerry made a gagging sound. Sometimes Lila made me gag too. She and Ellen are Jessica's best friends—other than me, of course. But sometimes Lila brags too much!

"Let's hear where some of you are going tomorrow," Mr. Crane suggested.

Amy Sutton waved her hand. She and Todd are my best friends, other than Jessica. "I'm going to the TV station with my mom. They're thinking about giving her her own show!"

"Wow! Can I be on it?" Lila asked.

Amy shrugged. "I'm not sure. I think it's for grown-ups."

"I'm going to help my dad at his restaurant," Eva Simpson said.

"I wouldn't mind going to your dad's job," Lois Waller said.

"You'd eat all the food before they could serve it," Charlie teased.

"I'm sure we'd *all* want to eat Mr. Simpson's food," Mr. Crane said, giving Charlie a stern look.

"What are you twins doing?" Winston asked. "Going to court with your dad?"

"Your father is a lawyer, right?" Mr. Crane asked.

Jessica and I nodded.

"Hey, maybe they'll visit the jail," Charlie said.

"And get locked in," Jerry teased.

7

"Don't be mean," Jessica said. "We're going with our mom."

"She's been studying to be an interior decorator," I added.

"It'll be more fun," Jessica said.

"Sounds boring," Ricky said. "Looking at curtains and stuff all day."

Jessica frowned angrily. "It is *not* boring. Our mom just got a new job at Taylor's department store."

"We're going to be junior salespeople," I explained.

Jessica nodded. "We might even help Mom make a big sale."

"Who knows?" I shrugged. "Maybe Mom's boss will want to hire us this summer."

"Then we'd make lots of money." Jessica's eyes glowed with excitement. "We could use it to buy clothes."

I smiled. I'd never even thought of

that! If I made lots of money, I'd save up for my own computer. I'll need one since I'm going to be a writer.

"You twins can't sell stuff." Charlie sneered. "I bet you're gonna mess up big time."

Jessica sneered back. "Just you wait."

"Yeah," I added. "We'll show you." We were going to be the best salespeople the store ever had. And we were going to make our mom proud too!

CHAPTER 2

On the Job

The next morning Jessica and I rushed through breakfast.

"I can't wait to get to work," I said excitedly.

Steven wrinkled his nose. "I'm glad you goofballs aren't coming with me and Dad," he teased. "We have real important work to do."

Jessica stuck out her tongue. "Mom's job is important too. She takes care of people all day."

"And makes lots of big decisions," I added.

"Both jobs are important," Dad said. "Remember, Steven. You can't go into court with me. You'll be doing things around the office. Running copies, filing papers."

Steven frowned. "I thought I was going to help you with one of your big cases."

"Maybe next time," Dad offered. "But today it's office chores."

"*That* sounds boring," Jessica said. "We're going to have *fun.*"

A few minutes later we were in the car, riding with Mom to work. Jessica and I were so excited, we couldn't stop talking.

"I can't wait to see all the pretty stuff," Jessica said.

"I can't wait to learn about Mom's job," I added. "We're going to be great helpers. Can you teach us how to work the cash register, Mom?"

"Can we take the people's money?" Jessica asked excitedly.

"I'm good at math," I said.

"I know how to use a calculator," Jessica added.

Mom smiled as she steered the car into the parking lot around the Sweet Valley Mall. The mall looked bigger than ever today.

"I'm glad you'll both be spending the day with me," Mom said. "And it will be fun. But remember, it's a big store. There are lots of ways to get in trouble. I don't want you wandering off and getting lost."

"We're big girls now, Mom," Jessica said. "We won't get lost."

"And we won't get into trouble," I added. "We're going to be such good helpers, you'll want to hire us."

Mom laughed as she parked the car. "I hope so."

Jessica and I scrambled out of the car. We followed Mom up the sidewalk, through the big revolving doors into Taylor's, and up the escalator to the Home department.

A tall lady in a dark red suit and high heels greeted us. Her straight black hair was pulled back into a bun. She wore small square glasses that were balanced on the tip of her nose.

"She's tall," Jessica said. "I bet she has to bend over to go through doors."

"Shhh!" I hissed. "She might be one of Mom's customers."

"Well, she looks like a big red hen," Jessica said with a giggle. "Or an ostrich."

"That's Mrs. Hengstler," Mom said. "She's the Home department manager. And she's also my boss."

I pasted on a smile and stood straight and tall.

"Her hair's pulled so tight, it looks like her skin would hurt," Jessica whispered.

I nudged my sister's arm. "Smile, Jessica. We have to make Mrs. Hengstler like us. If we don't, we'll mess up like Charlie said."

Jessica straightened up, brushed down the skirt of her pink dress, and smiled the smiley-est smile I'd ever seen.

"Hi, Alice," Mrs. Hengstler said to our mom. Her voice sounded high and squeaky. "I'm glad you're here on time. Today's going to be really busy." She glanced at Jessica, then me. "What adorable girls!"

Mom put her arms around our shoulders. "Thank you. This is Elizabeth and Jessica, my twins. Since today is Take Our Daughters to Work Day, they're here to learn about my job."

Mrs. Hengstler smiled and glanced nervously around the store. "Yes, I remember . . . and I'm glad to have them. But we have a couple of important customers coming in today."

"Oh, I know that," Mom said, patting both our backs. "The girls will be fine. They're very well behaved."

"We're going to help," I said, beaming.

"I like stores and shopping," Jessica

added. "I'm good at picking out pretty colors."

Mrs. Hengstler pushed up her glasses and smiled again. But something about the way she was looking at me made me think I had toothpaste on my chin.

"You two look like good little sales-girls," Mrs. Hengstler finally said. "I'm sure you'll have a great time."

Jessica clapped. I felt like I had just won a contest. Mom's boss thought we were right for the job!

CHAPTER 3

Elizabeth's Coffee Break

"Welcome to Taylor's," Mrs. Hengstler announced before taking off to help a customer. "Have fun today."

Mom took two plastic badges out of the desk drawer. "Here. I made these store name tags for you."

"Cool!" Jessica said as Mom pinned a tag on her dress.

"Awesome!" I said. Our name tags were just like the ones Mom and Mrs. Hengstler wore. My tag had Elizabeth Wakefield printed in big black letters under the store's name. I was so proud!

Mom motioned for us to follow her. "OK, girls. Now you're official Taylor's employees. It's time for me to show you the Home department."

Jessica and I giggled at Mom's official-sounding tone. She was treating us like real salespeople!

Jessica roamed around, oohing and aahing over pretty paintings, frilly bed-spreads, and lacy tablecloths. I saw a cool dark blue blanket with glowing moons and stars all over it that I wanted to wrap myself in. But I knew I needed to stay close to Mom and pay attention in order to be a good worker.

Mom pointed to a wall covered with little hangers. Each hanger held a different-colored piece of fabric. The wall looked like it had been painted with a million perfect squares in a million beautiful colors.

"This is where our customers choose the fabric they want for their couches, chairs, bedspreads, and curtains. That way everything in the room will match."

"That white fabric with the pink roses is pretty," Jessica said. She crawled on top of a big stack of rugs. "Wow! I feel like a princess sitting up here."

"Why are some of the rugs hanging on the wall?" I asked.

"Those are authentic oriental rugs," Mom said. "They're very expensive and delicate. If everyone who came into the store walked on them, they'd wear out in no time flat."

After Jessica climbed down from her rug tower, Mom took us back into the warehouse. It was huge and gray and kind of dark. Big boxes were stacked up everywhere I looked. It was almost like a cardboard maze. I listened carefully as Mom explained how deliveries and special orders were received. I wanted to learn everything I could today.

Our next stop was the office. Mom's desk was right next to Mrs. Hengstler's. Mom had a big picture of me, Jessica, and Steven on her desk and a big sign that read Alice Wakefield for everyone to see.

While Jessica spun around in Mom's desk chair, I walked over to see what Mrs. Hengstler was doing. She was talking on the phone, so I peeked at some sketches lying on top of her desk.

She had drawn a beautiful dream bedroom. Everything matched, even the carpet. She had drawn a huge canopy bed right in the middle. I loved it! It looked like a fort. I could hide there and write poetry, read, or be by myself whenever I wanted.

I tried to ask Mrs. Hengstler who her drawings were for, but she kept talking and sipping her coffee. She set down the cup but not the phone.

"I'm ready to get to work," Jessica said. She picked up a clipboard, spun over to me like a ballerina, and bumped my arm.

"Ouch!" I grabbed the desk to keep

from falling. But I accidentally knocked over Mrs. Hengstler's coffee cup instead! Coffee sloshed out and ran all over her sketches!

Mrs. Hengstler slammed down the phone. "Oh, no!" she shrieked. "Look what you've done! You've ruined the bedroom design I just finished for a client."

"I'm sorry," I apologized, trying to wipe up the coffee with a tissue. But the more I tried to clean it up, the bigger the mess became.

"I'm sorry too," Jessica spoke up. "It was an accident."

"I'll have to start all over," Mrs. Hengstler said, shaking the damp paper.

I felt awful. I couldn't believe I'd messed up so soon!

Mom gave my shoulders a comforting squeeze. "Don't worry," she said. "We'll help Mrs. Hengstler clean up the mess."

Mrs. Hengstler glanced at her watch. "Never mind," she snapped. "I've got an important customer waiting. I'll deal with this later."

Mrs. Hengstler glided into the showroom, her heels clicking on the floor. Jessica gave me a caring look, and tears stung my eyes.

Mom hugged me. "Don't worry, sweetie. Accidents happen. I know you didn't mean to do it."

I shook my head against Mom's stomach. "I really didn't. But I'll make it up to her, Mom. I promise."

Mom brushed my hair from my face and smiled. "I know you will, honey. Come on, the store's starting to get crowded. Let's get to work."

CHAPTER 4
Princess Jessica

Jessica and I followed Mom into the Home department. About ten customers roamed around. Mrs. Hengstler was talking to a short, fat woman wearing green flowered pants and an orange top.

"Look at that lady," Jessica whispered. "She looks like a flowerpot with a carrot growing out of it."

"Shhh." I glared at Jessica. "We have to help Mrs. Hengstler and get her to like us again." I tiptoed up beside the customer and listened quietly while Mrs.

Hengstler told her all about furniture.

"This is a great store," I said with a smile. "Taylor's has the nicest furniture in Sweet Valley."

"And our mom works here too," Jessica added. "She knows all about decorating fancy rooms."

The flowerpot lady smiled. "Oh, my goodness. You're twins!"

"Yes, ma'am," Jessica and I said at the same time.

Mrs. Hengstler's stiff shoulders relaxed a little, and Mom winked at us. We were doing OK!

"You're adorable," the flowerpot lady gushed. She studied our name tags. "Elizabeth and Jessica Wakefield. I'm Dorothy Buttercutt."

"Pleased to meet you, Mrs. Buttercutt," I said, shaking her hand. Jessica did the same.

"Such well-behaved girls!" Mrs. Buttercutt declared.

"Yes." Mrs. Hengstler cleared her throat and grinned. "My top decorator, Alice Wakefield, is their mother. Perhaps she'll help you shop on your next visit."

Mrs. Buttercutt babbled on so loudly, I almost didn't hear the telephone ring. Mom answered it. While Mom was busy on the phone, I winked at Jessica. It was time to make our first sale!

"Mrs. Buttercutt, how do you like this sofa?" I asked, trying to remember how people acted in furniture commercials. "It's not only pretty, but it's comfortable too. See?" I sat down on the leather sofa and rubbed the arm. "It's really soft."

"And the beds are cool too," Jessica said, climbing up on a big four-poster bed and lying down. "I feel sleepy already, and I *hate* going to sleep." She closed her eyes and pretended to snore.

Mrs. Hengstler's eye twitched nervously. I wanted to tell her everything was fine, but Jessica and I were on a roll. Nothing was going to stop me now!

Mrs. Buttercutt brushed her hand over the leather sofa. "Well, it certainly looks comfortable."

"Check out this swing chair," Jessica blurted. She jumped off the bed and dove into the swing chair, setting it in motion. "Whee! It's just like being at recess!"

"Oh, my goodness," Mrs. Buttercutt said, fanning herself with her hand. "You're making me dizzy, child."

Mrs. Hengstler cleared her throat and shook her head slightly at Jessica. After Jessica slowed the swing, Mrs. Hengstler led Mrs. Buttercutt over to some lamps.

Jessica and I followed them, but Mrs. Hengstler shook her head no. "Why don't you help your mother?" she suggested.

We went over to see Mom, but she was busy on the phone and helping a customer at the same time. She didn't even see us peeking at her from behind a potted plant. Now that Mrs. Hengstler had shooed us away, we had nothing to do!

"I'm bored," Jessica declared. "Let's go play."

"I don't know," I said. "We're supposed to be working. If we get into trouble, then Mom might get into trouble too."

"Then we won't get caught," Jessica replied.

I groaned and followed her over to the fabric area. I hadn't noticed that there were huge, long pieces of fabric stored above the little tiny hanging ones. They were wrapped around long tubes that were set into the wall.

"Look at that shiny purple material!" Jessica climbed up on a stool and started pulling the fabric off the roll. It was like a big roll of shiny purple toilet paper. It kept unrolling until Jessica had a piece that was as long and wide as Mr. Crane's classroom.

"Stop!" I hissed. "Mrs. Hengstler's going to kill us!"

"No way," Jessica said as she wrapped the fabric around herself to make a shimmering gown. "We'll just hide it. She'll never know. Now fetch me my crown and my magic wand, squire."

I rolled my eyes. I knew that Jessica loved to play dress up and act like a princess, but I couldn't believe she'd do it in a store full of people!

"Fetch me my magic wand!" Jessica demanded. She pointed to a display of curtain rods.

"OK, OK. Anything to make you give up already." I wobbled and wove under the weight of the curtain rod. It was so heavy!

"Now bring me my crown, or I shall have ye thrown in the dungeon!" Jessica threatened. She was rocking back and forth on the stool, which didn't look too steady.

"What crown, O Spoiled One?" I asked. I grabbed a cardboard box that had been sitting on top of the counter. "Here. This should suit you just fine."

"How dare ye make fun of me!" Jessica cried. "Now I shall turn ye into a toad." She tried to raise her magic curtain rod, but it was too heavy for her. She dipped and bobbled and fell down with a crash! The entire roll of purple fabric came down from the wall and almost bopped her on her royally embarrassed head.

"Stupid throne," Jessica complained.

I laughed and laughed. She looked so funny sitting there on the floor that I had totally forgotten where we were and what we were supposed to be doing.

"*What* in the *world* was that?" I heard Mrs. Hengstler call.

"Jessica? Elizabeth? Are you OK?" Oh, no! *Mom!*

"Hurry!" I hissed. "Let's clean up!"

Jessica quickly began rolling the purple fabric out of sight. I put the cardboard box back where I'd found it and picked up the heavy curtain rod. But the second I put it back with the others, it fell over. It hit the tip of one of the other rods. Then the whole display toppled over. The rods crashed to the floor. They rolled around all over the place. One of the rods kept rolling and clinking all the way across the floor and came to a stop—right at Mrs. Hengstler's feet!

CHAPTER 5

Bumbling the Sale

Mrs. Hengstler angrily swiped at a strand of hair that had fallen from her tight bun. It seemed as if everyone in the store was right there staring at us, including Mom and Mrs. Buttercutt. I was so upset, I wanted to crawl inside one of the huge antique vases and never come out.

"We didn't do anything wrong," Jessica told everyone. "Honest. We weren't even playing or anything."

Mrs. Hengstler gave us a dark look, but she didn't say a word. She just led Mrs. Buttercutt back to the office.

Pretty soon everyone else had walked away—everyone except Mom. She gave us stern looks and told us to help fix the mess we'd made. I scrambled around, chasing and picking up the curtain rods as they rolled in all directions. Jessica crawled underneath a bed and grabbed the other two. Mom stacked them up neatly. Then she got a stockperson to help put Jessica's purple princess fabric back where it belonged.

When we finally finished, I touched Mom's hand. "I'm so sorry, Mom. We really were playing, and I was only trying to clean up."

"I know, honey," Mom said in a

sweet but firm voice. "But you really need to be more careful."

"I know," I replied guiltily. I remembered how Jessica had taken that big fall from the stool. She was lucky to be OK.

"I'm not always able to keep an eye on you both," Mom explained, "even though I try really hard. I thought you were busy with Mrs. Hengstler."

"She told us to go away," Jessica complained.

Mom ruffled our hair. "Well, you should have told me where you were going away *to*. And *I* should have been—"

"Yoo-hoo! I need some help!" a woman yelled.

Mom smiled politely at the customer. "How about you two go sit at my desk for a little while?" she suggested as she headed toward the customer. "Then I'll take you along on a sale. OK?"

Jessica and I nodded and sulked back to the office. It was pretty boring back there. But I guess Mom just didn't want us to get into any more trouble. I mean, it had only taken us about five minutes to get from helping Mrs. Hengstler to making a big stupid mess in the fabric area. That wasn't long at all! If Mom turned her back for a second, we could probably break everything breakable without even half trying.

I listened to Mrs. Hengstler and Mrs. Buttercutt talk. Mrs. Hengstler had spread out several pieces of fabric, and Mrs. Buttercutt chose a bright yellow one with blue and red squiggly lines in it.

"She sure likes wild things," I whispered.

"Yeah," Jessica agreed. "And I saw something she'd love." Jessica ran out of the office and came back in two seconds with a cool African mask. There were red, blue, and yellow lines painted all around the eyes and feathers sticking out of the top.

Jessica held the mask in front of her face. "Look, Mrs. Buttercutt!" she shouted.

Mrs. Buttercutt looked up and squealed. "Eeek! What is that awful thing?"

"It's a mask," Jessica said. "Isn't it wild? The colors match that fabric you like."

Mrs. Buttercutt leaned on the desk and pressed her hand over her heart. "You scared me to death!"

"Mrs. Buttercutt is interested in *French* styles," Mrs.

Hengstler said coldly. "The African mask does not match that style." She turned away and grabbed her calculator. "Now, let's total up your purchase."

I saw a furniture catalog on the desk and picked it up. I was good at math. Maybe I could help add up the sale! I turned the pages until I found the sofa Mrs. Buttercutt was buying. The price was three hundred and thirty dollars. I glanced at the tag Mrs. Hengstler was holding. It read three thousand, three hundred dollars. I checked the numbers in the book again. The tag must have been printed wrong!

"How much is it?" Mrs. Buttercutt asked.

This was my chance! I would tell Mrs. Buttercutt the right price and save Mrs. Hengstler's customer money. Then they would *both* be happy. "It costs three hundred and thirty dollars," I announced.

Mrs. Hengstler dropped her calculator. "What are you doing with that catalog?"

"I looked up the price for you. See?" I pointed to the price. "It says right here that the sofa costs three hundred and thirty dollars."

"*What?*" Mrs. Buttercutt gasped. "But it's marked three thousand."

"That price must be marked wrong," I said, using a businesslike voice like Mom's. I was really helping Mrs. Hengstler now!

Mrs. Hengstler's face turned red.

"Someone probably just put too many zeros on the tag price," I insisted. "I do it sometimes in math class."

"That price only covers *part* of the sofa," Mrs. Hengstler said sharply. She smiled at Mrs. Buttercutt. "It doesn't include fabric, cushions, or custom decoration. That means the one on the floor costs three thousand, three hundred dollars."

Mrs. Buttercutt snapped her purse shut and glared at Mrs. Hengstler. "Listen, I don't know if you're running a decorating center or a day care here. But I do know that I'm getting a headache."

"But—"

"We'll have to finish this another time." Mrs. Buttercutt shoved her chair back so it scraped the floor loudly and stomped away.

Mrs. Hengstler clenched her hands on her desk and blew out a steamy breath. "You have just bumbled one of the biggest sales of the month."

I gasped and dropped the catalog. What had I done wrong? I was only trying to help.

Maybe I wasn't cut out to work in a store after all.

CHAPTER 6
Mad Mrs. Hengstler

Mrs. Hengstler was so mad, her nostrils flared out. I stared at my shoes so I wouldn't look up her nose. I tried to tell her I was sorry, but Mrs. Hengstler wouldn't listen. She sighed loudly and called Mom into the office.

"I really didn't mind having you girls here," she began, "but I'm afraid you've been nothing but trouble all day. Double trouble."

Mom's eyebrows crinkled in worry. "I'm really sorry, Mrs. Hengstler. The girls have learned their lesson. I'm sure things will go better from now on."

Before Mrs. Hengstler could reply, a stout man with a bald head walked in. His dark bushy eyebrows met in the middle of his forehead. "I need to speak with someone in charge," he demanded loudly. He sounded almost as angry as Mrs. Hengstler.

"That's Mr. Schwister," Mrs. Hengstler whispered. "He's given us a lot of business. Girls, *please* try to behave."

Mr. Schwister pointed at Mom. "I came here looking for my special order. I expected it to be delivered yesterday!"

Mom smiled politely. "I apologize, Mr. Schwister, but we haven't found the package." She picked up a form from her desk. "It shows here it was mailed to us three days ago, but we don't have any record of receiving it.

There might be a problem at the warehouse. I can check."

Mr. Schwister's bald head turned bright pink under the lights. "You have misplaced my order! It was very expensive, and I've already paid for it . . . in *full*."

"He's being mean to Mom," Jessica whispered.

"Yeah," I replied. "It isn't her fault his dumb package got lost."

Mr. Schwister shook his finger in Mom's face. "If you don't find it today, you can pay for it and keep it!"

Mom simply smiled and continued talking in a soothing voice. "Mr. Schwister, I'm sure we'll locate it. If not, we'll place another order for you."

"But I wanted it *today!*"

Jessica leaned over to me. "He can't talk to our mother that way!" she whispered.

"How can Mom stand there and be so nice to him?" I asked.

Jessica and I started forward, but Mrs. Hengstler put her hand up to stop us. "Wait, girls. Your mom is fine. She's good at solving problems. And it's important for us to be nice to our customers even when they're not being nice to us. It's called being courteous."

"But he's being *awful*," Jessica argued.

"Your mom can handle it," Mrs. Hengstler said soothingly. "She's terrific."

I watched Mom, ready to pounce if Mr. Schwister said anything else. But it was just like Mrs. Hengstler said. Mom smiled sweetly, offered the man some coffee, and said she'd take care of everything. Mr. Schwister finally calmed down and sat in a chair, waiting.

"Mom *is* good," Jessica said. "I guess her job is a lot harder than we thought."

"Come on, girls. I have the perfect task for you." Mrs. Hengstler motioned for us to follow her. "It'll help me a lot. Let's go back to the stockroom."

Jessica and I trailed behind her until she led us to a pile of medium-size boxes. "We just received a large shipment of linen napkins. I need you to count how many boxes we received."

"Sure," I said with a sigh. The job didn't sound very exciting, but I'd do anything to make things OK with Mrs. Hengstler. How could I flop at counting?

"That sounds easy," Jessica said.

"It'll go fast with the two of you working together. Now be careful to double and triple check the number you get, and then write it down here." She handed me a notepad and pencil. "We don't want any more lost packages like Mr. Schwister's."

"Yes, ma'am," Jessica and I chimed at once.

"I'll get Marvin, the stock supervisor, to keep an eye on you." Mrs. Hengstler paused and looked at her watch. "It's eleven-thirty now. You should be done by twelve. And when you finish, why don't you take a half hour lunch break? You'll probably be starved by then."

Jessica and I nodded. My stomach was already rumbling. But work came first!

Mrs. Hengstler picked her way between the boxes to talk to Marvin. He had a nice smile and dark eyes that twinkled. His curly hair was short, and he wore a dark green work shirt with his name on the front.

"This sounds boring," I said to Jessica. "But I guess it's a pretty important job. After all, Mr. Schwister was really upset that his package got lost. Someone must have counted wrong."

Jessica agreed and started counting the boxes. I started counting too. But I couldn't stop remembering what I'd told Charlie yesterday in school. I'd bragged that I was going to be a great salesperson.

I'd been bragging just like Lila Fowler!

And so far I hadn't sold *anything*.

CHAPTER 7

The Wildest Warehouse in the West

Jessica and I counted and recounted until we got the same number—fifty-seven—about five times. We figured that had to be right. But when we looked up at the clock, it was only about eleven forty-five. We still had fifteen minutes till lunch—and nothing to do!

We went to ask Marvin for another task, but he suddenly got called away to unload a shipment off a big truck. We peeked out through the stockroom doors into the store, but both our mom and Mrs. Hengstler were busy.

One thing was for sure. It was time to go exploring!

Jessica and I poked around through the stockroom shelves until we found some beautiful, gleaming brass animal statues.

"Oh, cute!" Jessica said. She usually hates animals, but the statues were of dogs and cats. Plus they didn't smell bad or try to bite her.

"Maybe Mom could buy us one of these cat statues," I suggested. "It might be the only cat we ever get to keep."

Jessica sighed. "I know."

"Too bad Dad and Steven are allergic to cats." I groaned.

Jessica picked up a small, shiny lamp from the bottom shelf. "It's a magic genie lamp!"

"Let's make some wishes," I said. "I'll go first." I put my hand on the lamp and rubbed it. I imagined a genie popping out with a turban and everything.

I closed my eyes tight and concentrated. But I didn't have to think long. I knew what my wish was—to do something special to show Mom what a great businesswoman I could be.

"What did you wish for?" Jessica asked.

"I can't tell or it won't come true," I said, spotting an open box. I reached in and touched something soft. Something furry. Was it alive?

I pushed the packing pieces away and spotted an owl. It was covered with feathers and everything. "Wow. It looks real!" When I pulled it out, Jessica shivered.

"It's creepy. Those big eyes are staring right at me!"

"There's something else," I said, running my hand along the bottom. "It feels hairy."

"Oooh, what is it?" Jessica asked.

"It's pretty big, Jessie. Help me."

Jessica came over and helped me pull the hairy thing out of the box. She looked worried. "What if it's alive?" Jessica asked. "It could be another animal."

We pulled out a big, brown, furry rug. "It looks like bearskin." I dropped the rug and tried not to picture a big grizzly chasing me.

"Wow!" Jessica rubbed her fingers along the edge. "It's soft, but I wouldn't sit on it. It might bite me!"

Marvin walked over after the delivery truck left. He shook his head and stared at the rug. "I know that's fake fur, but I wouldn't want it in my house."

"I wouldn't either!" I agreed, glancing at the owl. It really seemed spooky sitting next to the hairy rug.

Marvin picked up the notepad with the number fifty-seven written on it. "Fifty-seven boxes of linen napkins. Good job, girls. Now I'm going to take my lunch break."

"Is it OK if we eat our lunches back here too?" I asked.

Marvin nodded and went into his little glass office, where he began to eat his lunch.

"Why do you want to eat back here?" Jessica asked. She wrinkled her nose.

"Because if we eat real fast, then we can go *exploring*," I replied.

"Awesome!" Jessica said. She dashed into the showroom and came back with our sack lunches.

"Did you tell Mom where we were?" I asked.

"Mom was still helping mean Mr. Schwister," Jessica said. "So I told Mrs. Hengstler we were going to eat back here. She said it was fine and that she'd tell Mom."

"Good," I said. We both climbed on top of a pile of boxes to eat. We wolfed down our tuna-squish sandwiches without even talking and gulped down our milk. Then Jessica grinned and pointed to Marvin's office. He was fast asleep in his chair!

We quietly jumped down from our perch and went through a few of the already opened boxes. "These foam things look like snow," Jessica said.

"Especially the way they're sticking to your clothes," I said.

Jessica threw a handful at me and laughed. "Let's have a snow fight."

The pieces landed in my hair. I grabbed a handful and tossed them at her. They stuck to her dress and arms. We brushed the pieces off, laughing as they dropped to the floor. We were laughing so hard, I was afraid we'd wake up Marvin. But he was out cold.

"Let's play hide-and-seek," Jessica suggested.

I spied some bigger boxes in the back. A great hiding place! "OK. Start counting."

Jessica covered her face and counted to ten. I scrambled away and slipped behind a box of pillows. "Ready or not, here I come!" Jessica called. I heard her footsteps as she skipped through the stockroom. As she came nearer I crouched down low, trying to wedge myself between two boxes. Suddenly the box with the pillows fell over. The pillows toppled out!

"I found you!" Jessica squealed.

I laughed. "No fair. The pillows gave it away."

Jessica pressed my hands over my eyes. "Now you find me."

I closed my eyes and counted to ten. "Ready or not, here I come!" I checked under the pillows, behind the boxes. She wasn't behind the cart. Not behind the door.

Then the big furry rug moved. Either the rug was alive or Jessica was underneath!

I picked up the corner and peeked below the rug. "I found you!"

Jessica squealed. "I'm glad you found me. It's hot under there. And scary!"

Suddenly I heard a strange noise. *Tap. Tap. Tap.* "What was that?" I whispered.

Jessica stopped giggling and clutched a pillow in front of her.

Tap. Tap. Tap. Something skittered across the floor.

We both let out little shrieks, then louder ones. Marvin didn't even wake up. But the weird noises continued.

Tap. Tap. Tap.

"Something's alive in here!" Jessica

gasped. "That spooky owl must be coming after us!"

Tap. Tap. Tap tap. Tap tap . . . It went faster and faster.

My heart pounded in my chest. Jessica and I clutched each other. "There's a ghost in the stockroom!" I cried.

CHAPTER 8

Mouse Madness

"Yikes! It's a mouse!" Jessica squealed. She crawled on top of the boxes, almost knocking me down.

"It's so tiny!" I knelt down to watch it. It was carrying a little bread crumb in its mouth.

"It's gross!" Jessica shrieked. "Get it out of here!"

"Stop screaming. I think *you're* scaring *it,*" I said. "And I don't think it's gross. It's kind of cute. It was hungry—see, it has a piece of your sandwich in its mouth."

"Yuck!" Jessica made a hissing sound. "I don't care. I don't like mice."

"It can't hurt you, Jessie. You're a hundred times bigger than it is." I quickly searched the room with my eyes. "I'm going to help it get out of here."

"Go ahead. But leave me out of it," Jessica said, clutching the edge of the box and backing up even farther.

I tiptoed closer to the mouse until I could almost touch it. The mouse's tiny ears stood on end.

"It's OK, little mousie," I whispered. "Don't be scared. I'm going to help you."

I moved slowly, but the mouse suddenly skittered away. I ran after it. It ducked behind a box.

"Come here, little guy. I won't hurt you," I said softly. "Here, mousie, mousie, mousie."

The mouse darted out and ran toward the back of the stockroom. I raced ahead to catch it. "No, mousie. The door's this way!"

It crawled around a statue and across one of the fancy rugs. Then it scampered inside a basket on the floor. I snapped the top of the basket closed so the mouse couldn't get out.

"I caught it!" I yelled to Jessica.

"Good." Jessica climbed down from her perch.

I looked at the mess we'd made in the stockroom. "We'd better clean this up before Mrs. Hengstler gets back."

"Yeah. Or she'll start squawking again like a mean mother hen."

I giggled at Jessica's joke, and we straightened up the boxes. While I restacked the pillows I'd knocked over, Jessica picked up the foam pieces.

"Hey, I found something back here," Jessica called. She came back carrying a package. "I've never seen stamps like these before."

"They're foreign," I said. "The package is a weird shape too." It was rectangular with a rounded top, and it stuck out on the sides.

"And look at that fancy writing." Jessica traced it with her finger. "I wonder where it came from?"

"Maybe it's something really cool, like a knight's dagger," I suggested.

"Or a princess's crown."

"Or it could be something scary—like an animal head."

"Yuck!"

"Or a voodoo doll," I said, remembering one I'd seen in a magazine.

"Yikes!" Jessica said. "What if it's dinosaur bones or a person's skeleton?"

Jessica and I traded worried looks. "I guess we should take it to Mom and Mrs. Hengstler."

Jessica nodded, but her hands were shaking.

"I'll get the mouse. We can take it out of the store where it'll be safe. Then we'll find Mom. She'll know what to do." I picked up the basket, and Jessica and I started for the door. But Mrs. Hengstler stopped us before we could make it out of the stockroom.

"What are you two up to?" She glanced from the basket to the mysterious package. "You're supposed to be finishing your lunch."

"Well, see—," Jessica started.

"Yes, I *do* see," Mrs. Hengstler said. "I see you're playing."

I opened my mouth to explain, but Mrs. Hengstler glared at me. I knew she wasn't going to listen to anything I had to say.

Then suddenly the basket swayed. The mouse was crawling around inside!

"I'll take that basket, young lady." Mrs. Hengstler grabbed the basket from me and swung around. The basket swayed again.

I reached out to steady it, but Mr. Schwister walked up and cleared his throat loudly. When Mrs. Hengstler lowered the basket to the floor, the basket swayed again. The top came off—and the little mouse scrambled out!

CHAPTER 9

The Mystery Package

"Eek!" Mrs. Hengstler jumped backward and grabbed Mr. Schwister's arm.

"Yikes!" Jessica jumped onto a nearby chair. The mystery package was still in her arms.

The mouse ran in circles around Mrs. Hengstler's feet before crawling underneath one of the chairs in the corner.

"What in the world is

going on?" Mr. Schwister asked. "I don't know what kind of place you're running, Mrs. Hengstler. It's bad enough that you've lost my package. But now you've got mice in the store!"

Mrs. Hengstler's face turned so white, I thought she was going to pass out. "I don't know where that *thing* came from!" she shrieked.

"I was only trying to take it outside," I began, but then Mom ran up. Her face was red and flushed, and she had tears in her eyes. "Where have you girls been? I've been searching all over for you! I was so worried you had gotten lost."

"Didn't Mrs. Hengstler tell you we were working in the stockroom?" I asked.

"No!" Mom cried.

"Didn't she tell you we were eating

lunch back there too?" Jessica asked.

"No!" she cried again.

Mrs. Hengstler looked down at her feet. Her face turned from white to red in about two seconds. "I'm sorry, Alice," she apologized. "I meant to tell you, but it's just been so busy."

Jessica and I traded confused looks. Everything had gone wrong now!

"These girls are troublemakers," Mr. Schwister declared, pointing to us. "*They* brought the mouse into the store. I demand an apology."

"We weren't trying to make trouble, honest," I explained.

"Elizabeth was trying to take the mouse out of the store, not bring it in," Jessica added.

"Really?" Mrs. Hengstler asked.

"Yes," I replied. "We were all finished with our task, and Marvin took our sheet. Then we ate lunch. And then we found the mouse. I knew you wouldn't like having a mouse in the store. I was only trying to help by taking it outside."

"And then when I took the basket away from you, the mouse came out," Mrs. Hengstler said. "Oh, this whole mess is my fault. It sounds like you two were working hard back there."

"We were. We even cleaned up after ourselves," I said.

Mrs. Hengstler smiled. "That's super. You two are pretty responsible after all."

"You sure are," Mom told us. "I'm proud of you."

"We even found this weird package," Jessica said, holding it out for everyone to see. "It was hidden behind some boxes. It didn't look like it belonged there."

Mom squinted at the package carefully, and then her eyes went wide. "Oh, my goodness!" she gasped.

CHAPTER 10

Hired or Fired?

I twisted my hands nervously. I was afraid Mom was going to get angry at us for snooping around. But instead of being angry, Mom sounded excited. A big smile grew across her face.

"What is it?" Jessica and I asked at once.

"Yes, what is it?" Mrs. Hengstler asked. She sounded just as curious as we did.

"It's Mr. Schwister's missing package!"

"You're kidding!" Mr. Schwister said. His big belly shook with laughter. "I don't believe it!"

"No, look. The funny stamps and writing are from China. It's the mirror Mr. Schwister ordered." She grinned at Jessica, then at me. "And you girls found it! This is wonderful."

"You two really saved the day," Mrs. Hengstler said. "Thank you."

"You're welcome," Jessica and I said at the same time.

Mr. Schwister cleared his throat again. "I guess I owe you girls an apology. You were a big help. I really shouldn't have gotten so upset at you or your mom." He patted us on the back. "Today's my wife's birthday, and she's been wanting this mirror for a long time. Thanks, girls. Now she'll have a happy birthday."

Mom hugged us both, and we grinned back and forth at each other. "You did a great job," Mom said. "I wish I could bring you to work with me every day!"

We hugged Mom, and Mrs. Hengstler walked over and patted our shoulders. "Girls, I'm sorry I've been so cranky today. I guess I had too many things to do, and I let it get to me."

"It's OK," I said with a smile. "We really *wanted* to help. It just didn't always come out right."

Mrs. Hengstler chuckled. "And you did help," she said. "Thank you . . . for everything. You know, it's been really nice having you girls here today." Mrs. Hengstler's smile grew bigger. "I have an idea. As a reward, you spend the rest of the day designing your own dream rooms for a window display."

"Wow!" Jessica gasped.

"Cool!" I exclaimed. "How do we do it?"

"I have a special computer program that'll help you," Mrs. Hengstler explained. "It will let you choose whatever furniture and fabric and colors you want."

"That'd be awesome," Jessica said.

"I love working on computers," I added. I couldn't wait to begin! I already knew I wanted a canopy bed so I could hide out in it and write. And a striped bedspread. I knew Jessica's dream room would be full of pink, frilly things.

"I know you're going to have fun," Mrs. Hengstler said softly. "And you're going to do a great job. I have a feeling you're going to become fine businesswomen someday—just like your mother."

Mom grinned. "I know they will. They're both smart girls."

"Thanks, Mrs. Hengstler!" Jessica and I said at the same time.

I ran over to Mom and hugged her. I felt closer to her than ever. "Take Our Daughters to Work is a lot of fun," I said. "But it's a lot of work too. I never knew how hard your job was until today."

"Yeah," Jessica chimed in. "I can't believe you do this during the day and take care of us too!" She smiled mischievously. "I can't wait to tell Lila about designing my dream room. She's going to be so jealous."

"I can't wait to tell Charlie about our adventure," I said. "He won't believe that the Wakefield twins saved the day!"

"Yeah, he'll never make fun of us again." Jessica giggled.

Mom and Mrs. Hengstler traded confused looks.

"Who's Charlie?" Mrs. Hengstler asked.

"Just some dumb boy," Jessica said. Then Jessica and I laughed so hard, Mom and Mrs. Hengstler joined in.

**Turn the page for
great activities from
Elizabeth and Jessica!**

Jessica's Wild Word Search

Jessica wrote down ten of her favorite words from the story. Then she hid each one either horizontally (side to side) or vertically (up and down) in the word search puzzle at the bottom of the page.

Can you find all ten? Good luck!

CANOPY	MONEY
CURTAIN	PILLOW
FABRIC	RUG
LAMP	SALE
MIRROR	WAREHOUSE

```
H  P  U  M  W  P  W  A  B  O  N  B
C  U  R  T  A  I  N  T  W  G  I  M
V  Y  T  M  Q  L  X  U  A  W  H  I
F  S  D  F  I  L  B  W  R  X  T  R
E  A  N  A  M  O  R  Y  E  U  P  R
B  L  P  B  T  W  F  V  H  S  K  O
L  E  J  R  I  C  A  N  O  P  Y  R
D  Y  P  I  Z  F  J  L  U  A  M  P
I  H  B  C  S  R  T  N  S  O  T  W
X  Y  M  O  N  E  Y  J  E  K  L  R
V  I  P  N  W  V  S  R  W  R  U  G
P  L  A  M  P  F  H  O  C  P  S  X
```

Elizabeth's Cool Crossword

Elizabeth remembered ten things that happened in the story. But after she wrote them out, she erased a word or name from each sentence!

When you figure out what the missing word or name is, fill in the blanks. Then you can write the missing word in the matching crossword spaces!

Can you get all ten words right without peeking back at the story? Good luck!

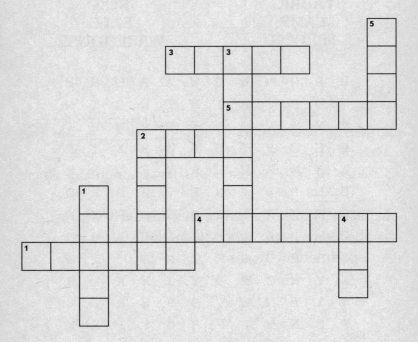

ACROSS

1. Elizabeth said she wanted to be a _____ when she grew up.
2. Jessica put on an African _____ at Taylor's.
3. The twins thought they found a magic _____ lamp in the warehouse.
4. Jessica thought Mrs. Hengstler looked like an _____.
5. Jessica wrapped herself in _____ fabric at Taylor's.

DOWN

1. Mr. Schwister's mirror was from _____.
2. Jessica was scared of the _____ in the warehouse.
3. One of the twins' jobs was counting linen _____.
4. Elizabeth liked the statue that looked like a _____.
5. The twins were working in the _____ department at Taylor's.

Answers

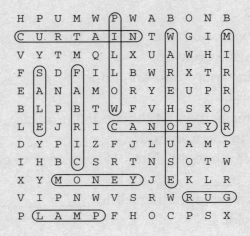

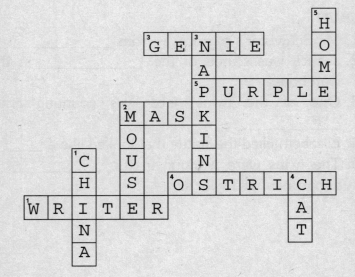